MW00935589

An Adventure of Scribble Dog and Pointy Fox

An Adventure of Scribble Dog and Pointy Fox

Written by Frank Warren

Illustrations by Harriett Noel

☾ BrookTree Media ✳ Takoma Park ☆

An Adventure of Scribble Dog and Pointy Fox

Copyright © 2021 by Frank Warren and Harriett Noel

ISBN: 978-0-9979423-9-2   (Hardcover)

Cover and book design: John W. Warren
Cover and Interior Illustrations: Harriett Noel
Design consultation: Heather Williams

Published by BrookTree Media
Takoma Park, MD

Printed in the United States of America

for all the
Grandchildren

❀ ❀ ❀

This book sits

Quietly on the table

Waiting to be read

(and colored if you wish)

☆ ☆ ☆

Scribble Dog and Pointy fox live in oregon on the bank of the North Umpqua River. Scribble Dog has a custom-made log house, and Pointy fox has a cozy den under a big cottonwood tree.

The two furry friends were not related but shared the same riverside territory and had grown up together.

Their favorite sport was chasing wild turkeys and deer along the grassy bank. The deer were too fast and the turkeys quickly flew up into the trees, so the two scamps could never catch anything big.

They almost caught a black tomcat, but it scrambled up a telephone pole at the very last second.

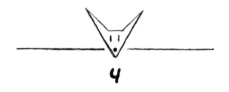

Scribble Dog and Pointy Fox wore coats of curly-gray and brownish-red fur and were about the same size, knee high to a pony. Pointy was bigger and taller than all the other oregon foxes because his grandfather, wily frank coyote, was larger than any fox. Since Pointy was part coyote, he too was wily and smart. Sometimes he was too smart and outfoxed himself!

On a late summer afternoon the two furry friends were looking for something good to eat. They had nibbled on some yucky cat food at a nearby house and both still had an odd fishy taste in their mouths.

"Let's go over to the other side of the river, Scribble. I overheard the river geese saying the blackberries are really good this year," said Pointy.

"How can we get over there? The river is too wide and deep to swim across," said Scribble.

"We can trot across the railroad bridge, downstream. No problem," assured Pointy Fox.

"What if a freight train comes along while we are up there on the bridge?" asked Scribble.

"This is Sunday, silly dog. Trains never run on Sundays. Let's go!" urged Pointy.

The two trotted down river and up the steep bank to the railroad bridge. The railroad trestle was very high over the North Umpqua River, and they would have to watch their step during the crossing.

Pointy Fox went first and trotted easily along the rails at a foxtrot pace. Scribble Dog loped along right behind him. When they were halfway across the long bridge, Scribble heard a

🌀 "TooT! TooT!" 🌀

"Was that a train ℰTᴏᴏT! TᴏᴏT!℘ I just heard?" yelled Scribble.

"What else goes ℰTᴏᴏT! TᴏᴏT!℘ besides a train?" answered Pointy, looking over his shoulder.

"Step it up!" Scribble Dog urged. "Here comes a freight train, Sunday or not!"

Both were trotting along as fast as they could foxtrot and dogtrot but still had a way to go to the other side. Suddenly they knew they were not going to make it across in time. "Let's jump into the river," urged Scribble.

"It's a long way down to the water. Can you swim?" asked Pointy.

"My mom taught me to dogpaddle when I was a pup," answered Scribble.

Both leaped off the high railroad bridge just as the speeding train zoomed by.

🍥 🍥 "TOOT! TOOT!" 🍥 🍥

There were two huge splashes as they hit the river.

They bobbed up to the surface like corks, and the soggy doggy and frantic fox paddled quickly to the opposite bank.

"Did you see any big hippos or ugly crocodiles out there in the river?" asked Scribble Dog.

"No, not today," said Pointy Fox. "I guess we are just two 'Lucky Dogs.'"

"Let's go find those sweet, juicy blackberries. I'm starving!" said Scribble, shaking the water out of his fur coat.

"Ok. We'll dry out on the way," replied the waterlogged fox.

A little way upriver they found lots of wild berry bushes with big clumps of juicy, ripe blackberries hanging down.

Yum. Yum.

The two ate their fill at the ALL-YOU-CAN-EAT Blackberry Festival and then lay down on the grassy riverbank for an afternoon nap in the warm sunshine. About five o'clock they each opened one sleepy eye to see if the other one was awake.

"Time to head back home, Scribble," yawned Pointy Fox.

"How are we going to get back across the river, Pointy?" asked Scribble.

"Same way we got over here, only in reverse, and without a dip in the river," laughed Pointy.

"What if that freight train comes again?" said Scribble Dog, in a worried tone.

"We'll listen to the rails and keep our ears perked up," assured Pointy.

"ok. Let's go. The worst that can happen is that we'll have to jump for it again," said Scribble.

"Right," agreed Pointy.

The travelers made their way back to the railroad bridge, up the embankment, and started carefully back across the river, listening for a train's

❦ "TooT! TooT!" ❧

They foxtrotted and dogtrotted hurriedly along on the steel tracks without any problem and made their way home again at sunset, just as the orange moon was rising.

It was always great fun to howl at Ulumquh, God of the Moon, when the big full moon came up over the dark hills.

🌀"Yoowl, Yoowl, Yoowl, Yip, Yip, Yip"🌀
howled the two furry friends.

About the author:

Frank Warren, a lifelong resident of California, relocated recently with his wife, Mary Jo, to Roseburg, Oregon. The Scribble Dog stories were originally written twenty years ago for their two grandsons, who lived on the North Umpqua River and still do. Upon moving to the North Umpqua River in late 2020, Frank resurrected the stories.

About the illustator:

Harriett S. Noel is a graduate of the Art Institute of Pittsburgh where she studied Advertising Illustration. She is an artist and designer who also resides on the North Umpqua River. Her art includes work in acrylic, watercolor, pen and ink, and scratchboard.

About the font:
In publishing, a font is what the book designer uses to display the text. The font used in this book is called "Good Dog" (appropriate, right?) and it is designed by Fonthead Design (Ethan Dunham).